Many thanks to my editor, Jennifer Arena, who suggested New Orleans as Fred's hometown, and to my insightful agent, Jennifer Carlson. I am grateful to April Whatley Bedford, Interim Dean, College of Education and Human Development at the University of New Orleans, and to Louisiana librarians Terrence E. Young, Jr., MEd, MLS, Jefferson Parish Public School System, and Anna Campos (recently retired), St. Ann School, for their kindness in reviewing the story. And a huge thank-you, as always, to Christopher and Christy.

To Jana, a big fan of crawfish and pralines
—M.Q.

To my brother Javi and my friend Marta.
Thanks a lot for your support. It gave me the courage I needed.
To my mom, my dad, and my brother David. I'm so proud of you.
My most sincere thanks to Jan and Justin.
To Claudia and Marcos. I love you.
—P.C.

Library of Congress Cataloging-in-Publication Data
Quattlebaum, Mary.
The hungry ghost of Rue Orleans / by Mary Quattlebaum ; illustrated by Patricia Castelao.
p. cm.
Summary: Fred the ghost is perfectly happy haunting his ramshackle New Orleans house until Pierre and his daughter Marie move in and turn the house into a restaurant.
ISBN 978-0-375-86207-6 (trade) — ISBN 978-0-375-96207-3 (lib. bdg.)
[1. Ghosts—Fiction. 2. Haunted houses—Fiction. 3. Restaurants—Fiction.] I. Castelao, Patricia, ill. II. Title.
PZ7.Q19Hu 2011 [E]—dc22 2010037063

MANUFACTURED IN CHINA
10 9 8 7 6 5 4 3 2 1
First Edition

The Hungry Ghost
of Rue Orleans

By Mary Quattlebaum

Illustrated by Patricia Castelao

RANDOM HOUSE 🏠 NEW YORK

FRED LIVED ALONE AT 28 RUE ORLEANS. Once the house had been a jazzy-snazzy, sweet-and-spicy spot, but now? The floors squeaked, the roof leaked, and dust coated the chairs.

But Fred liked his rickety house. All night he moaned and clicked his fingers and tended his tiny cactus. If he got hungry, he gobbled some air. The perfect life for a ghost.

One day, Pierre and
his daughter, Marie,
barged through Fred's
broken door.

"Our new restaurant!"
they shouted.

"My house!" Fred
cried.

But no one heard.

Pierre banged nails
and washed stairs. Marie
swept away cobwebs. They
polished windows and
painted walls.

"Nooooo," Fred wailed.
But no one heard.

In came tables,
chairs, and a giant
stove.

"No more!" Fred
stomped his wispy
foot.

But no one heard.
Trucks arrived
with celery, peppers,
and paprika spice,
crawfish, onions,
red beans, and rice.
Then such a noise!
CHOP, whisk,
sssss . . . sssss, whisk,
CHOP.

One evening, quiet settled over 28 Rue Orleans, and
Fred heard a different sound.

Clank.

Had Pierre and Marie left? Had a new ghost moved in?

Fred slipped down the polished stairs, past the gleaming
stove and . . .

CLANK, CLANK, CLANK.

Twenty forks rattled like ghost chains.
Twenty people shook their napkins, raised their
glasses, and dined upon gumbo, crawfish, and
red beans and rice.

"Welcome to our restaurant!"
Pierre shouted.
"My *house*!" Fred hollered.
But no one heard.

Now Fred was tired of no one hearing. This place, so horribly spick-and-span, no longer *felt* like home. His beloved dust—gone. His squeaks and leaks—gone. His cobwebs—gone.

Who had invited these munchers and clankers?

They needed to go!

And before you could say "hungry ghosts gobble air," Fred began to moan. **Ooooooo.**

He tossed the gumbo. **SPLAT!**

He juggled the crawfish.

Whoosh-whoosh!

He flipped the red beans and floated the rice.

Flip-flip-FLOOOOO!

The diners cheered.

"Ahem." A portly man coughed pompously. "I must, I simply *must*, comment on this food and this, er, *strange* performance."

Conti, the critic! He loathed everything: butter balls, carrot curls, pralines, and pie.

Marie held her breath. Fred rubbed his hands happily. He'd soon have his home back, for sure. Conti would *hate* a haunted restaurant.

"The food is spiced nicely and served up with style." The critic dabbed his lips. "But this show, this *mysterious* show"—he threw out his hands—"makes this restaurant an OUTright, OUTrageous, five-star . . . SUCCESS."

Conti beamed at Pierre. "A ghost makes your restaurant unique."

Fred hid behind the stove for the next few nights, but still the diners came.

CLANK, CLANK, CLANK.

"Enough," said Fred sadly. "I must find a new home." So he packed his valise and hoisted his cactus.

"Good-bye," he moaned from the door. But as he turned, his plant pricked Marie.

The girl stopped her hurry and scurry. "Are *you* the ghost?"

"What did you expect?" said Fred tartly. "A floating sheet?"

"I thought you were steam from the kitchen," said Marie apologetically. "And you speak so softly. Now I can tell you've been here all along. Wait, are you leaving?"

"You took my home," said Fred, opening the door.

Pierre whisked by with a special dessert. "My masterpiece!" he cried. "Powdered Ghost Puffs."

"Named for me?" asked Fred.

"This is the ghost," Marie told her father. "We took his home."

"Oh, no!" Pierre dropped the beautiful puffs.

Fred caught the tray and . . . sniffed. Ah, that smell! That wonderful powdery-sugary smell! It smelled like 28 Rue Orleans on a bright and busy, jazzy-snazzy day.

Fred picked up a dainty puff. "Why, it's light as air," he said.

"Your house!" said Pierre. "We are so sorry."

"Would it be possible to share?" asked Marie.

"Absolutely not." Fred took a teeny-tiny bite. "I need squeaks and leaks and dust. This place is nothing but clean and gleam and shine."

What to do? Marie pondered. Pierre puzzled. Fred nibbled another puff.

And another.

And another.

"Oof." He gazed at the last puff. "Do I have room for one more?"

"Room for one more," Marie slowly repeated. Then she smiled and dashed up the stairs.

For the next three hours, Marie banged and thumped while Pierre kept Fred busy with puffs.

Finally Marie led Fred to the broken door and he saw the sign . . .

FRED

He could hardly believe his eyes.
Dust everywhere.
Squeak went the floor.
A slow drop dripped from a leak.
"My own room!" cried Fred. "Let's
celebrate with Ghost Puffs."

Marie and Pierre named their restaurant The Hungry Ghost. And 28 Rue Orleans became, once again, a jazzy-snazzy, sweet-and-spicy spot.

If you ever visit, listen *ve-e-e-ery* carefully. Right after the eight o'clock ghost show, Pierre offers dessert in Fred's private room. What's being served? Powdered Ghost Puffs, of course!

CLANK, CLANK, CLANK.

A Note from the Author

A big bowl of gratitude goes to the city of New Orleans, where I've enjoyed delicious meals, delightful strolls, lazy river trips, and snazzy jazz. I didn't want to try to replicate, duplicate, or in any way infringe on the city's own lively Orleans Avenue or any of the restaurants and guesthouses located there. Rue Orleans is a fictitious street, and 28 Rue Orleans, where Fred lives, is not based on any specific house or restaurant.

The city's cuisine deserves a huge dollop of thanks. In fact, I couldn't decide whether the restaurant should feature Cajun or Creole dishes— and so, you might notice, both types are served. As for the Powdered Ghost Puffs, they were inspired by New Orleans's delectable beignets.